Delinquency Lessons

stories by David Essig-Beatty

Big Black Bird Books
509A Judyville Road
Lewisburg, WV 24901

While the places and events described in this book are based upon real ones, the characters are entirely fictitious. Any similarity to real persons, living or deceased, is coincidental and not intended by the author.

Cover photo from Beatty archives with permission, crow © Scott Streit (www.bird-friend.com) with permission.

ISBN 978-0-578-01744-0

Contents

For my mother Beatrice Reed Beatty who kept us together despite being uprooted and my father James Franklin Beatty who endured the Depression, a world war, and a large and sometimes troubled family.

Delinquency Lessons

Three Crows

Three crows tumble from a bluing sky,
talons entwined,
beaks glistening,
toward a rock-strewn stream:

First up is fish crow
flapping from a sycamore
for the day's forage at Raritan Bay;

Next your garden variety
drops from an oaken perch
high above Chimney Rock;

Then a northern raven
drafting above First Watchung
dives into the fray.

Three crows peck and flap,
peck and flap, peck and flap
tumbling along the basalt hillside
inured to the certainty
that one will thrive,
another survive,
a third die
in the tumbling waters of the Middlebrook.

- Enzo Januzzi, 1976

Lesson 1: Button Your Lip

"Wiley Weed" I lisp into the silence of the first day of kindergarten.

"Well Mr. Riley Reed" greets the teacher "get out of those muddy clothes and into this", handing me a clown costume and pointing to the closet at the back of the room.

"Not Wiley, I'm Wiley Weed" I explain to giggles echoing around the wooden-floored room at LaMonte Elementary School.

"I don't care if you're Lyndon Baines Johnson, there's no filth in my class."

———

I was covered in mud because hurricane Beulah circling out in the Atlantic Ocean had just drenched central New Jersey. In the hills of Eastern Kentucky where my Reed family had lived since the early 1800s it had never rained for six straight days. My father had dragged us out of the family hollow and up to Bound Brook four years before for his truck-driving work.

On the first day of school I was supposed to follow my brother and two sisters but Blaine ran off with his friends as soon as the house was out of sight. I kept up with Beatrice and Beulah until we came to the playground.

"Did you know this park is named for Thomas Codrington?" asked a big kid sitting in the middle of the merry-go-round.

"Huh?" I replied, pushing off and hopping on as Beat and Beulah headed down the sidewalk around the park.

"He bought it from the Lenne Lenape in 1683 and built the first house on an Indian mound" he continued as we creaked to a slow spin.

"Indians here?" I marveled.

"The tribe had moved west to join the Shawnee but a few stragglers swindled the British gentry" he concluded as a sixth-grader ran up and started circling the rusty iron wheel.

There was nothing to do but hang on so by the time the merry-go-round slowed enough to jump off the girls were gone.

Two big black birds caught my eye flapping over the baseball field and there they were walking up Evergreen Avenue toward Old Ladies Hill. The thought of having to pass by the haunted mansion alone spurred me to try to catch up by cutting across the park instead of following the girls around on the sidewalk.

"That mound is under Old Ladies Hill" called the big kid as I took off across the outfield.

The first running step onto the mushy infield claimed my right sneaker. I was able to retrieve it by balancing on the left foot and thrusting both hands deep into the orange muck. Forging ahead, I managed to keep both shoes on by slowly lifting them straight up with each step, only falling once more. My sisters were halfway past the creepy old mansion by the time I caught up.

"I declare, if it in't Wiley the mud monster come to scare off the haints" teased ten-year-old Beat in her not yet abandoned Appalachian accent.

"Whyncha roll in the grass to clean it off" offered Beulah with her jet black hair and deep blue eyes, looking out for her freckled-faced little brother.

I just kept walking to get past those scary old people rocking and staring from the big front porch so most of the mud remained as I arrived at the kindergarten door.

―――――

"Much better Riley" assures the teacher as I try to sneak into a little desk at the back of the room.

"Some getup Weeds" hisses a tall lanky guy at the next desk.

"Bound Brook gets hit by a hurricane once every twelve years" whispers that chunky guy from the playground who's now sitting right in front of me.

"That why they call you Newsy?" mumbles the tall guy, christening Enzo Januzzi with his nickname.

"Leo Mazurkevich, there will be no private conversations at the back of the room" grumbles the teacher.

I just sink down into my chair.

Lesson 2: Run Fast

"Pull down your pants" commands Dicky Dick pointing his sharpened
stick at my six-year-old sister Beulah.

———

We had ventured down to the brook for the first time without our big siblings. The square-mile borough of Bound Brook is aptly named and its western boundary is the Middlebrook. This clear running creek springs in a Y from between First and Second Watchung Mountain, east-west volcanic spurs from the Appalachian uplift that cut across central New Jersey to within sight of the coast. The two forks of the brook meet at a gap below Chimney Rock before tumbling a mile south along the edge of town and into the Raritan River. Just about every neighborhood adjoins one such sycamore lined stream and each stretch is claimed by the nearby kids.

A big black bird flew up from the railing as we crossed the Union Avenue bridge and headed into the dense late summer woods along a narrow trail on the western rim.

"Stay close, this is the path to the Poop Hole" advised Beulah.

I gladly complied, staying at her heels and humming the Four Seasons hit Walk Like a Man as we skirted a spooky old ditch. We were edging past the top of a dirt slide when surrounded by the group of whooping boys.

———

"His too, his too" chime the Campbell kids, moving around to see as Dicky Dick pokes his stick into my belly.

Fumbling with my zipper I break into tears.

"Run" shouts Beulah as she yanks me back and takes off down the trail.

We race for the bridge with the Crescent Drive kids in hot pursuit, barely making it to the safety of the road.

"They won't be coming back to our woods" assures Beulah when we're close to home.

Neither would I, I thought.

Lesson 3: Look Before You Leap

"Third try for a new world record" I huff pacing in front of the orange rosebush. My spindly five-year-old legs had just failed twice at emulating the long strides, flying leap and two foot landing I'd seen Ralph Boston do in the long jump of the 1964 summer Olympics.

———

The roses were at the end of their flowering season in my mother's yard of shrubs. First out in spring had been roses-of-Sharon which she calls "rosasharn" in her eastern Kentucky lilt. The light green buds made great pellets for pelting sisters from behind the bushes planted at intervals around the house. Any remaining buds unfurl into white or lavender whirls much loved by bumble bees and Reed kids.

"Betcha can't catch one" challenged Beat, daring Beulah and me to crimp the petals around a fat black and yellow bee.

"Let's hit her with our bee bombs but don't forget to run" whispered Beulah as we took off after our big sister waving the buzzing buds.

The last flowers out in the fall would be chrysanthemums with their own distinct pleasures. Pinching a tight green ball of a bud between thumb and finger unfurled a tiny burst of crimson. The survivors would become soft knobs emitting the bittersweet smell of Indian summer.

In between the rosaharns and mums came the real roses. Their tapered buds hid deep colors revealed as burgundy, white or flame by unpeeling the green outer petals. Our mother didn't trim the bushes so their tendrils arched outward hanging with fragrant sweet-tart bunches that called in the Japanese beetles.

"You can crunch em like this" explained Beulah showing me how to pinch the brown and green shells. "Mom'll give you a penny for each one."

"OK" I lied, launching a handful of the scratching bugs up into the air.

"A petal will pop if you hit it like this" Beat demonstrated, placing one over a circle made by her thumb and index finger and slapping it with the other palm.

But my favorite flower game was leap rose to the chagrin of the gardener.

———

A big black bird flaps up from the roof as I speed toward the bush and jump, sending petals and a red sneaker flying before tumbling down with thorn-ripped pants.

"Way to go Bleeds" cheers a red haired kid from the lilac bush across the street mistakenly thinking I was pretending to be my brother the high school quarterback and linebacker.

Lesson 4: Talk Tough

"Hey Weeds, call her fuckincunt" advises Leo Mazurkevich as my twelve-year-old sister Beat walks by kicking up orange and red leaves. I shout the mysterious word from behind a hedge. Two big black birds fly up from the maple tree as she turns back toward home.

"I showed her, dint I?" cackles Mazurk.

———

I like hanging out with my first grade classmate despite Mom's warning that "he's a bad egg." He's the middle kid in a large Polish family piled into a box-like house just like ours in Bound Brook's newly developed west-end Downs Manor neighborhood. The blond Mazurkevich boys ruled the middle section of the loop of Hanken Road.

Mazurk and I turn our taunts toward the Calavito girls playing in their yard across the street until I hear Beat's two-handed whistle, my signal to come home. Dad had promised to take us to Silver Saddle Ranch. Our Uncle Loy owned the place and would pop open green bottles of Coca Cola from the big red machine after we rode his horses. I hadn't ridden alone and thought this might be the day.

My father had followed his oldest brother to New Jersey in 1960 for work in Loy's trucking company, leaving Mom in Kentucky with us four. Nine months later, shamed into retrieving his family by his own mother, Dad piled the three older kids into a makeshift living room at the back of an old tractor-trailer, helped Mom up into the cab with me on her lap and carted us out of the southern Appalachians with the back gate of the trailer propped open for air and light. By 1965 he was barely supporting our family of six by driving all week and fixing up trucks on the weekends.

————

Hearing Beat's too-wheet into her cupped hands I start to hop on my rusty red bike but Mazurk grabs the handlebars.

"Stand on your seat and pull that handle" he commands pointing to a little white box sitting in the middle of a red stripe up on a telephone poll in front of his house.

"I can't reach it" I lie, afraid to stand on the bike.

"Sombitch, guess I'll hafta."

I hold the handlebars while he steps up onto the seat, stands on tiptoes, and tugs the handle as he jumps. A loud bell rings out from the box so we scatter, Mazurk around his house into the backyard and I peddling as fast as I can. I'm nearly home when a fire truck comes blaring by.

Beat smirks as I open the kitchen door.

"C'mon you girls" blurts Dad standing up from the table.

"He aughta go too" says Mom turning from the sink to see tears streaming down my cheeks.

"Shut your bigodamouth, I ain't takin no cursin sonovabitch" spits Dad as he stomps out to wait in the car.

Lesson 5: Run Away

"Hey Kenfucky, betcha can't hit the road" taunts Mazurk from the playground across the street.

"Don't worry about him, just stick with me" whispers Newsy before calling out "this basalt is a volcanic rock from the Haelig quarry at Chimney Rock."

"No shit Sherlock" laughs Mazurk climbing up the monkey bars.

———

Newsy and I had been heading down to the park when waylaid by the gravel pile. The gray hunks had been dumped into an inverted cone in a newly cleared lot.

First we raced to the top for king of the hill, sliding back down and climbing up again. Next we tumbled the biggest rocks down from the top. I belted out "King of the Road" from the then popular Roger Miller song and that's when Mazurk issued his dare.

———

"The colonial army camped where the quarry is now in the winter of 1777" continues Newsy as he tosses a stone underhand through the branches.

The impact on the blacktop sounds like a roll of caps.

"You Guineas throw like girls" chides Mazurk straddling the bars.

I heave the next one as high as I can. Three big black birds flap off as the rock shoots through the leaves, arches over a telephone wire and crashes down with a shattering of glass. We freeze as the car screeches to a halt.

"Hey you kids, get over here" screams a man jumping out of the car.

 In the ensuing silence I look at Newsy, he looks at me, and we leap down the back of the hill.

We're sprinting down Grove Avenue with hearts pounding until Newsy pulls up. I glance back to see him being spanked and hit the dirt track of Tea Street full tilt, finally turning onto the newly paved Hanken Road. I think I'm in the clear as the gate to our chain link fence clangs closed behind me but then I hear the slap of shoes on the blacktop. Running around the house, I slip into the back door and scoot under my sisters' bunk beds.

A loud bang at the screen door startles my mother from the nearby washroom.

"You get away from my house" she cries, slamming it in his face.

18

"But where's that boy who broke my windshield?"

"There's no boy in here. Now get outta here or I'll call the cops" she yells before retreating upstairs to lock the other doors.

My breath returns as I hear the guy walking away. I hide under the bed as long as I can stand it, finally reasoning that Mom might never know if I pretend nothing is wrong.

"All right mister, just wait till your father gets home" she warns before returning to the favorite of her shows As the World Turns.

I pack up my plastic Army mess kit and hit the road.

Running away from home would have normally meant hanging out at our stretch of the brook but I'm afraid those Crescent Drive kids might still be there. So after the mess kit is packed and the canteen filled I sneak out the back door and head around the half circle of Hanken Road humming "no food, no phone, no pets, I ain't got no cigarettes" until coming to the end of the loop. Left is Tea Street and the quickest way to home and my father's belt. Straight ahead is the cracked car. I turn right into the old west end of Bound Brook.

I had heard Blaine talking about Italian and Polish gangs in that part of town so my heart is racing again as I tear through briers to get to the familiar gurgling of the brook. After skipping a few flat red stones I leap from rock to rock until my PF Flyers are soaked. Exhausted, I sit down on the ledge of a concrete sewer, wolf down the Charles Chips and lemonade, and try to decide where to spend the night. Crawling into the sewer pipe might work but I'd heard Beulah say there was a dead cat in there. I think of following the brook down to the trestle by the river but remember Blaine describing a huge snapping turtle who lived there.

"Snap" from the bushes jerks up my head.

"Creak" descends from a sycamore.

"Caw-caw" from overhead makes me jump.

"Go home, go home" whispers the Middlebrook.

My father's old mint green 1959 Oldsmobile wagon is sitting in the driveway. I creep along the house and Mom catches me peeking in the kitchen door.

"Come and get it" she yells and I flinch as my father strides past. He just settles into his seat at the back of the table as my brother and sisters pile around. I creep in to the kids table and sink into the little chair expecting the yelling to start at any moment. It never does and those are the best chicken and dumplings ever.

Lesson 6: Use Your Head

"Hut one, hut two, hike" I shout to no one in particular at halftime of the Bound Brook Crusaders high school football game at LaMonte Field.

———

Before the game I had climbed the home team bleachers with my father and two sisters. Dad stood on the top bench chain smoking in his truck driving greens. Beat jumped down off the back of the rickety wooden seats to play with her friends. Beulah scampered down through the scaffolding to scrounge around under there. I sat next my father and watched the players in their red and white uniforms warming up by pushing a two man blocking sled across the practice field. Once the game started I occasionally glimpsed Blaine's number nineteen among the jumble of players. Mostly I watched the big black birds circling over the sunny south slope of First Watchung Mountain beyond the field and thought of the other game earlier that week.

"Someday you'll be better than Bleeds" shouted my second grade gym teacher Mr. Gramicelli across the blacktop after I returned the opening kickoff for a touchdown. What he didn't know was that I was really running from Mazurk who had given me my first taste of football violence the weekend before by slamming my nose into the ground with a spinning tackle in Tommy Greenwood's backyard.

Mr. Gram had just initiated schoolyard football by making me captain of one team and Mazurk the other. His first pick was Y.A. Yanetta so I took Tommy. Next he nabbed Jerry Brownell so I countered with big Newsy. Then it was back and forth until all the second grade boys were split. All, that is, except Stephen Perhach who could neither punt, pass, nor kick, much less run. I took him so the game could get started.

Claiming the quarterback position to stay out of Mazurk's grasp, all I saw when I dropped back to pass was a scramble of boys. He was equally inept as the other quarterback so the game was tied at one touchdown when Danny Gram called "time for one more play." We huddled at midfield to plan our last stand.

"Hit me over the middle, I'll take it in" offered Tommy.

"Nah, Mazurk'll pick it off" I reasoned.

"The screen pass is designed to trick aggressive defenders" stated Newsy.

The play unfolded beautifully with Mazurk and the others flowing right with Tommy and Newsy, leaving Stephen all alone on the left sideline. The ball hit his hands, popped up toward the goal line and landed in soft fingers as the whistle blew.

"Shit, see you guys down the park" yelled Mazurk.

———————

At halftime of the BBHS game I run over to the practice field and line up in a three-point stance in front of the blocking sled, leaning onto one hand with my red Keds planted. "Hike" launches me head first into the padded metal post. When I come to the sky is spinning and there's a sharp pain at the top of my neck. I feel like I'm going to throw up as I stumble back to the bleachers. My father lights up a Chesterfield as I lie down on the wooden bench.

"Big girls, they don't cry-y-y" sings Beat mimicking the nasal whine of Frankie Valli's 1965 hit.

"Wiley, I found a five dollar bill, let's go to the snack stand" calls Beulah from beneath the bleachers.

But even the prospect of hot chocolate doesn't make me stir.

After the game Dad drives us downtown to Efingers, steering me past the hanging bucks and mounted eel to the football section. I wobble past stacks of shoulder pads and helmets to baseball where I pick a black and orange Baltimore Orioles cap.

Two weeks later my sixth birthday present is a red and white football uniform.

Lesson 7: Smash the Snake

"That's my fish" cries Tommy Greenwood as I back away from the water dragging in something big. He had tripped running for the pole and his bloody nose convinced me to grab the reel before it was pulled into the brook.

"It's yours" I say with relief, handing over the rod as whatever's on the other end writhes in wild figure eights.

———

We had decided to go fishing that spring when Tommy had gotten a rod and reel for his birthday. On our next family shopping trip to Great Eastern Mills I had shown my father a Zebco spincast set I was eying over in sporting goods. He inspected the sealed plastic pack and then led me over to a bargain cart, picking out a saltwater rig and a little jar of salmon eggs.

The next day Tommy and I met up at the lilac bush.

"What kinda rope you got on that thing?" he asked.

"It's for big fish" I lied, embarrassed by the thick tan line and extra large hook.

"My Dad says the biggest ones are down by the trestle" he advises.

Sure enough we spotted a long green fish sitting in a pool beneath the railroad tracks. Tommy cast his plastic worm as I threaded the huge hook with bright pink eggs which went flying off with my first cast. I ended up dropping the baited line into the pool from up on the tracks in between Tommy's casts under the bridge. The big fish just sat there with an occasional wiggle of its side fins.

"Try a bread ball on a baby pin" advised Beulah the next time we went down the brook.

I did and snagged one from a silver-sided school shimmering around the pin.

"That's just a shiner, a worm'll getcha a real fish" laughed a teenager from across the brook.

A few nights later bare-footed Beulah came charging into the rec room from a spring shower with a big grin.

"Eeuw, I squished something slimy out on the sidewalk" she laughed.

We scrounged up a flashlight and found hundreds of nightcrawlers

26

wriggling in the puddles. They were fast and slick but we managed to fill a milk carton before the flashlight died.

———

"It's a water moccasin" Tommy exclaims as the dark green thing thrashes over the rocks tangling itself in the line.

"Nah, it's an electric eel" proclaims Jerry Brownell, leaping back as it squirms up a white-barked sycamore sapling.

"The American eel is a catadromous fish born in the Sargasso Sea but living in rivers before returning to salt water to breed" states Newsy.

"Where does he get this shit?" asks Mazurk as three big black birds flap down into the branches.

"The elvers used to swarm up the Raritan but their numbers declined when Calco started making aniline dyes to replace German plant dyes during World War I" continues Newsy unperturbed.

"Shut the fuck up and help" curses Mazurk bending down to lift a boulder.

Lesson 8: Run Faster

"Just wiggle it out a little to let you get away" advises Beulah.

But that longer fuse didn't buy enough time to escape the flying slugs.

The goods had arrived from West Virginia that June tucked under the sleeper in Dad's green and tan Apgar's truck. He divvied them out around the kitchen table, a half dozen chipped Homer Laughlin plates from his load to Mom, a carton of sparklers for Beulah and me, and a case of firecrackers for Blaine and Beat to sell for a dollar a pack. The silver sparklers were good for a few nights of streaking across the yard, spelling out names, or short-lived duels decided by the last one to drop a searing wire. Then Beulah pilfered a pack of Black Jacks from Beat's stash.

"Wiley, light this for me and I'll throw it" she instructed from behind the shed.

The skinny gray fuse was bent down so I held the match to the top to avoid burning the black and white firecracker. I pulled away when the fuse sizzled and she whipped her arm back and threw just as a loud crack exploded in our ears.

"Ooh, it got me" she hissed, afraid our mother would hear from inside the house.

We ran to the hose and I sprayed her swelling finger until the pain eased.

"It's just a blister" she decided handing me another firecracker. "Your turn."

"I saw a bunch of slugs under Buff's house when I was digging worms."

———

We tilt back the pink dog house our father had built from wood scraps gathered from around the yard and shingles he had hauled for Ruberoid. Grabbing a slimy black and gray slug in each hand, we plop them in the middle of the yard. Two more trips and there's a pile of twelve writhing gastropods.

I hold the Black Jack in one hand, grasp the bottom of the fuse between thumb and index finger, and wiggle it out a quarter of an inch. Then I slide the firecracker down into the gooey mass.

"Happy birthday to you" sings Beulah standing up on Buff's house as I light the tip of the fuse and take off across the yard.

I make it half a dozen strides before getting pelted in the back by burning mollusk flesh.

"Eeuh" laughs Beulah pinching her nose to the putrid stench enveloping me and the yard for the rest of that week.

Lesson 9: Stash the Loot

"Meet at the lilac bush after school to rob the Food Fair" commands Beulah. Newsy and I are glad to comply since our last attempt had gone sour when the stash of Bit O'Honey was discovered by ants.

———

Beulah and I are veteran shoplifters, having raked the Jew Joint (aka the Park Luncheonette) for my baseball cards and her Sweet Tarts for more than a year. After refining the buy-one-lift-one routine under the watchful eyes of the owner, a pale guy with concentration camp numbers stamped on his forearm, the big grocery store would be easy pickings. Beulah is a rangy black-haired fourth grader who had given Tommy Greenwood a bloody nose the year before in a battle for the lilac bush. The huge old shrub between properties had an open area in the middle that neighborhood kids used as a fort, clubhouse, home base and all-around meeting place.

———

The next day Beulah and I wait surrounded by the dark green leaves and remnant purple smell.

"No Newsy's good news" she chuckles after half an hour. "Let's go."

I'm crawling out humming "These Boots are Made for Walking", a hit song by Nancy Sinatra that year.

"Wait, what's the plan?" she asks calling me back into the lilac bush.

I only shrug.

"We'll zip some pies inside our jackets and walk out the back door" she decides.

A big black bird caws from up on the big twin Fs as we march through the front doors, past the cash registers, and down to the pie aisle. There they are, TastyCake, Dolly Madison or Hostess, fruit, cream or glazed in row after row. It's hard to choose.

"Come on Wiley, pick one before somebody sees" hisses Beulah slipping a Dutch apple pie into the front of her jacket.

34

I grab a coconut cream and slide it up under my coat. We're side-by-side heading for the back door when yanked back.

"Where do you think you're going with those pies?" asks the store manager with a sly smile.

"What pies?" Beulah replies.

"Zip down your coats" he spits.

I do and mine breaks open as it hits the floor.

"What are your names?"

"Wiley We-" I blurt, cut short by Beulah's "hush!"

"I'm gonna call the cops" he says while dragging us by our coats toward the office.

As I break into tears Beulah slips out of her jacket and takes off for the back door. The manager lunges and that's when I pull free and run for the front exit.

The automatic doors slow me enough to notice Newsy coming in as I head out. I run down Union Avenue and see two big black birds cruising toward the Codrington Apartments. I follow and the chase proceeds with me in the lead, the manager huffing behind, and Newsy taking up the rear. With heart pounding and lungs burning I turn a corner and scramble into a sunken window ledge. I hear his keys jingle past and think the coast is clear. Then the keys return and suddenly stop. I peek up to see a wicked grin as the manager reaches down to drag me out.

He's leading me by the collar back through the apartments when Newsy catches up.

"Mister, did you know these apartments are named for the town founder?" he asks walking backward in front of us.

"Get out of my way" shouts the guy.

Our third grade friends Jerry Brownell and Y.A. Yanetta are riding past and hop off their bikes to join in Newsy's pleas. The guy is kicking them away when Beulah comes running around a nearby apartment, freezes in her tracks, turns white, and shoots back behind the building. In his moment of distraction I shake loose again and take off for dear life.

This time I don't look back until across Tea Street and splashing through the brook into unknown woods. Jogging down a wide trail that loops through the dense brush and crosses similar paths, I soon realize I'm on the fabled tank trails. Older neighborhood kids whispered stories about getting lost in this swampy maze left over from National Guard training during World War II. The trails are about six feet wide with brambles spilling over and deep rutted tracks filled with muddy foul-smelling water. I had just pulled myself out of a muck hole when I saw two men up ahead with traps dangling from their belts. It was either slink back toward recapture or chance an encounter.

They whirl in surprise and then laugh at the mud covered boy cowering before them. At first I'm relieved to recognize them as older kids from Hanken Road.

"What are you doing following us, stealing our traps?" one of them accuses.

"Nah, got caught stealing a pie from Food Fair" I whimper.

"I know a kid who went to reform school for taking a piece of bubble gum from there."

"How do I get outta here?" I sob.

"C'mon, we'll show you the way" says the other guy.

I follow the brook back to my neighborhood singing "one of these days these boots are gonna walk all over you." Then I cut through a backyard to avoid Union Avenue where I'm sure police cars are lined up. Worried the manager has found our house, I hide in the shrubs next door and wait. Shortly after the Calco whistle signals quarter to five and the end of day shift at the Cyanamid factory Beulah comes walking down Longwood Avenue. I pop up from the bushes so she joins me.

"I ran all the way past the high school and came back through the park" she explains.

"How did he know?" I whisper.

"There musta been a two-way mirror over the meat coolers."

"What'll we do?"

"Never go in the Food Fair again" she concludes.

And for the next five years until the store closes Beulah and I disappear whenever our mother yells "Which a you young'uns is goin to the store?" to the chagrin of our big sister Beat.

Lesson 10: Talk Trash

"Let's go Wiley, the garbage truck's coming" shouts Beulah over the television.

"Yes!" I yell jumping up from Fractured Fairy Tales.

———

Garbage cans were always loaded, I mean really loaded on the first trash day after Christmas. The previous year we had tried raiding them in front of houses but were chased away. This year we had plotted to follow the truck to see what the garbage man dumped into the trash smasher, hoping to grab anything good before it was swallowed up.

————

Three big black birds flap over the truck as we run out to the road. The driver is wearing a Santa hat and tosses us a couple pieces of Bazooka.

"Nice grab Weeds" laughs Newsy from the passenger seat.

He climbs down and joins us at the back of the truck.

"My old man's at the wheel" he explains. "He started throwing candy to German kids from his tank after the liberation of Dachau."

A little Italian guy in dirty oversized greens gives us a wink from a ledge on the side of the truck as it moves out to the next house.

"Ze King, rut tut tut ta, ze Premier, rut tut tut ta, zen all ze ministeres ..." I chant.

"Dude, that's the 1959 Harveytune La Petite Parade" exclaims Newsy.

"... Army, rut tut tut ta, Navy, rut tut tut ta, and Department Sanitaire" we all sing as the truck pulls up to another set of cans.

"Standa back" the guy warns, swinging one up and dumping it in as we crane to see.

He reaches into the trash with black rubber gloves and flashes a toothsome smile as he hands Beulah an Etcha Sketch dribbling gray powder from a crack across the front.

40

"Ze King, rut tut tut ta, ze Premiere, rut tut tut ta, zen all ze ministeres ..." we continue down the block as the crows swirl over the back of the truck.

Pinching his nose with one hand, the guy lifts out an old Childkraft encylopedia with a little purplish ketchupy stuff dripping from it.

"Here, here" claims Newsy to no objections as Mazurk joins the march behind the truck.

"...Army, rut tut tut ta, Navy, rut tut tut ta, and Department Sanitaire ... Boom ... Plop" we conclude pulling up to the last house on the loop.

Amid tissue paper, cardboard boxes, and kitchen scraps an electric football set tumbles into the dumpster of the truck.

"No!" Mazurk and I scream as the garbage man reaches for the flush handle.

"It's mine" we both shout.

"You'll play for it" Beulah decides.

We sneak the ratty box into our rec room, dump the contents onto the floor, and plug in the metal field. I line up eleven red players on one side, Mazurk the white players on the other. Beulah flips the switch and twenty-two little men buzz into a big dent at midfield, starting a slow skittering circle.

"It's yours" we say simultaneously.

"For Department Sanitaire" Beulah laughs.

Lesson 11: Go For the Throat

"Get the fuck off our field" demands Heinze DiGiampaolo from the front of a row of fifth grade boys marching onto the field as three big black birds settle into a sycamore in the pool-side endzone. He's the pudgy red-haired leader of a pack of Italian kids from the west end neighborhoods of Bound Brook.

———

I had shied away from tackle football at Codrington Park although I sometimes hid in a juniper hedge beside the field and watched the pickup games. The older kids looked so big and rough that I stayed in that haven of pee-green scent and blueish berries.

But in fourth grade Y.A. Yanetta emerged as my baseball card collecting friend and classroom rival. We raced to be the first to answer questions and were usually opposing quarterbacks on the school playground. When he said "let's meet down the Park after school" I took it as a challenge so we fourth graders played every day once Detroit beat the Cardinals in the 1967 World Series. Our knock-down drag-out games started on the way home from LaMonte School and ended when the quarter to five Calco whistle signaled the end of dayshift for fathers and time for kids to go home for dinner.

————

"But we were here first" reasons Y.A. as Mazurk, late for the fourth grade game, walks up behind the fifth graders.

"I said get the fuck off" growls Heinze.

"Yeah, you little kids gotta move over to the baseball field" chimes in Jimmy Randazzo.

"Did you guys know Old Ladies Hill used to be the mansion of George M. LaMonte?" asks Newsy.

Heinze heaves a tight spiral which we all turn to watch whiz past Newsy's head. A choking sound spins us back toward the fifth graders where Jimmy Randazzo's feet are dangling six inches off the ground. His face goes from red to white to blue as Mazurk's forearm tightens around his neck.

"OK, OK, it's us against you for the field" concedes Heinze.

My first play is a pitchout to Mazurk who's nailed in the backfield. The next two plays are incomplete passes as I have to scramble and unload the ball. After our punt Jimmy Randazzo takes the helm for the fifth

44

graders and picks apart our man-to-man defense with his left handed down-and-outs. Then Heinze catches a screen and brushes off a diving tackle before rumbling in for the first score.

They're up three to none when we huddle after a kickoff.

"They're walking all over us" groans Y.A..

"C'mon you pussies, help me make some tackles" shouts Mazurk.

"LaMonte came here when his wife's Wheatland plantation in Virginia was overrun in the Civil War" continues Newsy.

"Weeds, you move to receiver, Mazurk to center, Newsy to fullback so I can get you guys the ball" directs Y.A.

He takes the snap from Mazurk who knocks down the rusher and gets open for a ten yard pass. Next Newsy takes a handoff up the middle and drags Heinze ten yards before being wrestled down. Then Y.A. hits me streaking across the field on a post route for our first touchdown.
On the kickoff return Mazurk slams down Jimmy Randazzo who coughs up the ball. On our first play big Newsy lumbers up the middle carrying three fifth graders in for our second score.
Soon the game is tied at four touchdowns when the Calco whistle blows. The fifth graders slink off for dinner but we dance around under the big sycamore in the endzone which is full of big black birds staging for their dusk flight up to First Watchung.

"Fuckinay, we did it" shouts Mazurk.

"The LaMonte's donated the land for the park, school, library, and football field" concludes Newsy.

"It's our field now" asserts Y.A. staking our claim. And it is for the rest of that magical fall.

Lesson 12: Coordinate Lies

"Yeah, I'll only burn down by the brook" agrees Tommy Greenwood to Y.A.'s demand that we not light fires in the dry leaves on the way. I'm the only one to see that Tommy's fingers are crossed.

———

He's my red-haired friend from the Hanken Road cul-de-sac named Welsh Road but called "the circle". The winter after the botched pie robbery he and I had turned to Christmas bulbs, sneaking two from each string around half the block, popping some in the circle after school the next day, hiding the rest in his father's old toolbox, and hitting the other side of the block that night. Our stash had grown to over a hundred when one popped in Tommy's hand. The shard pulled out but the blood wouldn't stop so he had to tell his mother. Christmas was over by the time his stitches and grounding were done.

The next fall we stumbled upon some older guys from the neighborhood, sixth graders, floating burning rafts of sticks and dried leaves down the Middlebrook. At school the next day we recruited five classmates to try it out. We agreed to meet at the park that afternoon and that's when Y.A. issued his warning while we waited for our match supplier.

———————

"I hadda wait till my old man left" huffs Mazurk running up with an entire carton, ripping off the paper, and holding out the cardboard box.

"He's on the night shift at Carbide" he explains as we stuff our pockets with packs of matches labeled West Brook Inn.

The town was surrounded by factories which later became superfund sites: Union Carbide's PVCs; Cyanamid's aniline dyes; Johns Manville's and Ruberoid's asbestos. My father hauled for them all in the days when truckers unloaded their own toxic loads.

We head for the brook gathering sticks and singing "come on baby light my fire" which had debuted on Ed Sullivan the Sunday before. Tommy torches a pile of leaves under the Union Avenue bridge while the rest of us launch flaming rafts until the fuel is spent.

"Where's Fuddy?" asks Jerry Brownell about our classmate from the west end who had missed the meeting at the Park.

"Let's cut through the woods to get him" I suggest.

48

"We don't know the way" cautions Y.A. insisting on taking Tea Street to get to Fuddy's house.

"It's shorter down the path" opines Tommy.

"Fuckinay" concludes Mazurk.

A line of fourth grade boys climbs the rock wall next to the bridge and hits the trail along the ditch, winding through a ravine, past the poop hole, and up onto an open field crunching through the cedar-smelling leaves.

"The Minutemen must have set up a look-out here above the only road up through Chimney Rock" observes Newsy.

"Here we go again" groans Tommy.

"That ditch was a breastworks for firing at the redcoats" he continues.

"Who do ya think ya are, Dick Tracy?" spits Mazurk.

"The poop hole must have been a fire pit for a sentry hut."

Three big black birds flap up as we're heading back into the woods when Tommy yells from behind "help, it's getting away." Orange flames sizzle in the dried grasses all around him. We race back and stomp on the clumps of fire but it spreads faster than our feet can move. Mazurk heaves a big rock onto the flames and a wall of white smoke shoots up stinging our eyes.

"A fire will go out if deprived of oxygen" huffs Newsy.

"Shut the fuck up and keep stomping" growls Mazurk.

Stumbling out of the ring of fire, we set to work on its edges stamping and jumping in a desperate dance with only Newsy scooping on handfuls of dirt. Then the whistle blows.

Bound Brook had a strange fire signal in the 1960s. A series of low whistles would moan from up on three huge wooden poles around town. The sequence indicated the street of the blaze so that firemen could head that way along with about half the town. From up in the woods we hear "ah-un-ah, ah-un-ah" and then a pause. That's enough to know it's going to be 2-4-6 for Hanken Road.

"They're coming" Y.A. cries and we scatter into the woods.

"Wait up, Weeds, wait up" pleads Tommy as I take off for the brook tossing matches along the way.

He catches me as I wade through the hip deep creek. We emerge in the west end as fire trucks blare down Tea Street.

"What are we gonna do?" he whines crouching in the brush beside the road.

"We should sneak down the park and pretend we were playing."

We're sitting on the merry-go-round watching billowing clouds of smoke above the houses when Y.A. and Newsy walk up. They had fled west from the fire and followed the highway back to town.

"Did anyone spot ya?" Tommy whispers.

"Nah, but we saw Louie DelleToro riding his Kawasaki 75 up there" answers Y.A.

"What happened to Jerry Brownell and Mazurk?" asks Newsy.

An awful silence settles over us along with the smoke as we contemplate the fate of our friends. Then they emerge out of the haze, hop the fence to the Kiddy Corral, and join us by the merry-go-round. Mazurk is scratched all over his face and arms.

"I had to yank him out of the briers" explains Jerry. "We saw flames shooting across the brook onto the houses."

50

"What'll I tell my Mom?" moans Mazurk.

"Tell her you got tackled into the bushes playing football" I offer.

"What if they catch us?" Tommy worries.

"Whadya mean us?" counters Jerry.

"Juvenile arsonists have often experienced parental neglect or family conflict" chimes in Newsy.

"You ain't no goddamn Einstein" sulks Tommy.

"We'll say we were smoking in the woods and Tommy dropped one" offers Y.A. to settle the issue.

————

The forest fire dies back that night after the woods completely burn. Only three houses have roof damage thanks to the Bound Brook Fire Department. My friends and I lay low the next few days in school but when the cops haven't shown up by Friday we think we're in the clear.

I'm playing downstairs on Saturday afternoon when Mom yells "Wiley, get up here." Anticipating chocolate chip cookies, I leap up the steps, turn the corner and freeze. Officer John Rotunno is standing in the kitchen.

The interrogation begins with "did you light that fire, son?" Choking back tears, I blurt Y.A.'s lie and watch in amazement as the policeman apologizes to Mom, hops in the squad car, and starts around the block toward the circle. It hits me where he's headed so I run for the upstairs phone. There's no answer at the Greenwood house.

"It's reform school if I get nailed again" whines Tommy on Monday at school. "Why'd you rat me out Weeds?"

The cop had confronted him with "your friend Wiley said you did it", thwarting our coordinated lies.

————

We all try out for Little League the following spring, sitting in the back row as coaches call out their picks. Y.A. and Jerry Brownell go to Domanski's Dairy with the green uniforms, Newsy to the purple Congers. Mazurk is picked by the black team, Research, Tommy Greenwood by the Elks in red. The last pick goes to the maroon Truckers and I jump up when my name is called. Then I see the coach and sink back into my seat. It's Officer John Rotunno.

Lesson 13: Spin Your Wheels

"Just fall out before it hits the road" warns Danny DiBennedetti helping Newsy into the inner tube as he tells us how to roll down the backside of Old Ladies Hill.

———

Danny and his black haired brothers lived in a little green stucco house at the back corner of the mansion's property. Their father was the Charles Chips man and always had a spare tire or two hanging in the back yard. The DiBennedetti brothers were rough and tumble kids who controlled the LaMonte Avenue section of town. Danny was in Beulah's fifth grade class, Sammy in third grade a year behind Newsy and me, and their little brother Pickle was in first grade.

I'd had a run in with them that fall when Pickle kept running into the middle of our fourth grade football game during recess on the school playground. After the third time telling him to get off the field I lost it, tackling the tough little boy, sitting on his chest, and shaking him a few times.

"The DiBennedettis are looking for you" warned Rita Cecchini as we piled into the hallway at the end of that school day.

"Oh shit" I murmured scrambling through bunches of kids and running down the back steps from our classroom.

I was out the schoolyard gate thinking I was in the clear when I heard "hey Weeds, get back here."

I took off down Second Street with Danny and Sammy in hot pursuit and Pickle taking up the rear. They gained on me when a car cut me off at LaMonte Avenue. Just as I started to pick up steam they were on me.

"Don't you ever touch Pickle again" yelled Danny striking the ground with the first punch as I managed to hit his arm.

"Yeah and stay out of our neighborhood" growled Sammy glancing the second punch off the side of my head when I turned, unable to block it with Danny holding my arms.

I avoided Old Ladies Hill after that until Newsy talked me into going up one cold Saturday morning in December when nobody else showed up for a football game at the park.

———

"George LaMonte invented safety paper for checks to send cash back to his wife's family in Virginia during the Civil War" marvels Newsy.

"Quit stalling" growls Danny.

Two big black birds caw from up on a hemlock as my big friend curls up into the sagging tube.

"He sold the invention to First National Bank and used the money to build their new mansion in Piedmont Farms" he continues as Danny shoves him off.

A big black Buick turns the bend heading slowly west down High Street as the tube wobbles and then picks up steam down the steep hill. The driver is a little old Italian guy with thick glasses stooped over the steering wheel and staring straight ahead.

"Jump Newsy, jump" Danny and I yell from up on the hill.

The tube hits the curb and bounces up into the side of the car as we charge down the hill. Newsy tumbles out as the Buick keeps right on moseying down the road.

"Romney Road, New Hampshire Lane and Wheatland Avenue are named for Mrs. LaMonte's town, county, and estate which are now in West Virginia" concludes Newsy brushing off his father's big work pants.

Lesson 14: Say a Prayer

"We'll check em at dawn" says Steven Perhach after we had set his three traps in the Middlebrook woods. To do so I would have to skip Sunday school at the Methodist Church.

———

Steven had no such dilemma. His family had attended Saturday mass at the Russian orthodox church in South Bound Brook. They and other Soviet émigrés had settled in central Jersey for proximity to the only American seminary for their native religion. Their strange church calendar had other perks for fifth grade boys besides Saturday services. One New Year's day Steven and I had dragged my family's Christmas tree from the curbside down to his house since their's wasn't until January 7.

My mother had also clung to her religion despite leaving it in eastern Kentucky for an unsaved husband in New Jersey. During the week she sang snitches from old hymns like "Surely Goodness and Mercy" while doing the wash or cooking. Sunday was her day of the Lord even if Dad had to work on trucks to make ends meet for our big family. But come Hell or high water, probably both in a town called Bound Brook, the young'uns were going to Sunday school.

––––––––

Knowing there's no reasoning with religion I wear my clothes to bed and sneak out before dawn humming the Rolling Stones lyric "here it comes, here it comes, here it comes, here it comes, it's just your nineteenth nervous breakdown." Steven emerges at first light and we hop his back fence onto the trail to the brook. A big black bird comes hopping out of the mist down the blacktop of Union Avenue and flaps off as we cross the bridge into the Bridgewater woods.

The first trap is hidden in the haze above the rock wall, its steel jaws nearly catching us as we crisscross the bank before stumbling upon it. There is nothing in it, not even the raw hamburger we had set out for bait. Trap number two is easier to find behind a fat tree growing up out of the ditch. It holds the huge hand of a sycamore leaf. Our last trap down below a burrow near the old dirt slide grips a grisly paw with three remaining toes. Glancing around nervously, we quickly pull out the trap and scamper home. Mom beats me there, just back from church.

"All right mister, no Sunday School, no Pop Warner" she preaches.

I'm moping under her rose bush when my big brother Blaine drives up to take me to the game.

"What are you eating under there?" he jokes.

"Under where?" I dutifully reply before bawling "She won't let me play."

"Get in there and suit up, now!" he roars.

———

The first snap slips through my fingers and I have to pounce on the ball making it second down and twelve yards to go for a first down. The second snap bounces off my palms but is recovered by our center so it's third and thirteen. The third snap squirts past my hands and is scooped up by our halfback Harry Johnson who's hit for a five yard loss. The coach signals time out and calls me over.

"Quarterback sneak on tap" he whispers while spraying pine tar into my palms.

"On fourth and eighteen?"

"They'll never expect it."

I walk up behind Mazurk, place my hands between his legs, and think "God help me hold it." Then I tap him in the groin to signal the surprise snap. The football hits my hands and sticks so I take off up the middle, cutting outside past the safety for a nineteen yard gain and first down.

An hour and three touchdowns later Blaine shakes me by the shoulder pads, looks me in the eye, and asks "how's that for Sunday school, Little Bleeds?"

Lesson 15: Cut Christmas

"Gee...zuss...krist" huffs my father, each syllable punctuated by a stroke of his ax into the Christmas tree.

———

Each year the winter holiday brought dread to our household along with the expected joy. Early in December Dad would shout that the lights were crooked as Blaine climbed a ladder and strung them along the outline of the house while Beat, Beulah and I peeked from behind the car. Mom would open an old Scrabble box containing a cardboard manger set for us to piece together and then complain that we put the sheep where the shepherd goes or that we set it on top of our best piece of furniture, the television set. Wrapped boxes would begin to bulge from beneath Mom's dresser despite her warning that it would be a lean year. The weekend before Christmas we'd pile into the Plymouth and drive to a tree lot beside Union Avenue Pharmacy, each offering opinions about shape, height and needle length.

"Just pick a godamn tree!" Dad would grumble.

"Why's he have to rush ya into getting that scraggly thing?" Mom would complain as she guilted Beulah into picking the cheapest one on the lot.

Dad would trim the trunk to fit it into our red and green stand, setting it up in the corner of the living room while hissing "hush your mouth, it's straight enough." He'd unwind the line of little lights, cursing each burnt out bulb before replacing it and looping them up and down the tree. She'd trim the branches with kitchen shears, snipping a wire to our muffled snickers on the down stairs and Dad's "stupid sonovabitch." Then we kids would layer on scratched bulbs and teardrops, red and blue chocolate balls, and strings of silver tinsel until the tree was nowhere to be seen. It reappeared the next morning as the decorations were rearranged in the night, some into order by our mother, others with red and blue foil into piles in the yard by our dog Buff.

––––––––

None of these glad tidings happen in the year of the ax. It snows on December 1 and Dad, home early after his truck-driving trip is cancelled, drives up with a big grin and a tall Frazer fir strapped to the roof.

"Why'd ya wanna get that thing so early?" greets Mom.

"C'mon kids, dig out the tree stand" he says ignoring her first complaint.

"It's dry as a bone" is the next volley while he shaves chips off the trunk. "The needles'll be all over my rug."

"Where's the real meaning of Christmas?" punctuates his wedging of the tree into the stand.

"I'll not have that ugly thing in my house" is the last straw.

Each chop invokes the Christ and evokes a gasp. After three blows we three kids slink away to our rooms to contemplate the end of Christmas.

———

The next three weeks pass without lights on the house, nativity in the living room, or mincemeat in the oven. On Christmas eve Dad is down at Apgar's fixing up trucks for a little extra cash. Mom's fiddling in the kitchen and fretting about not making it to church that night. As dusk descends we hear scratching along the side of the house. In comes our big brother Blaine just home from his first year of college at Rutgers and dragging a beautiful tall tree. He pops it into the stand, disappearing out the back door as Dad drives up. He just throws his coat in the closet and settles into his seat at the kitchen table for a silent supper. Late that night Blaine returns to take Mom and us kids to the candlelight service at the Methodist Church. The singing of O Holy Night at midnight has more than the usual melancholy in this year of no Christmas.

Blaine drives us home and we pile into the house to find a miracle: The tree is decked with strings of many colored lights and dangling ornaments. Mom reaches into a cabinet and pulls out a red box of silver tinsel, handing it to Beat before heading up to bed.

"Who fixed up the tree?" I ask lying next to Beulah on the living room floor watching the twinkling shadows of needles dancing around the ceiling.

"It must have been him" she marvels, "they're strung up and down like he always does."

"Will we get anything?" I wonder thinking of the electric football set I'd circled in the Sears catalogue.

"We just did" she whispers.

Lesson 16: Smell a Rat

"Ya can't run away from your troubles" my father says while looking across the yard to the incoming 7pm bus at the Union Avenue and Tea Street stop. We're both hoping that Blaine will get off.

———

Two days earlier a package had arrived from our sister Beatrice in Thailand. She had dropped out after her first year at Montclair State College to join the Peace Corps and was teaching English in Bangkok. The box contained a picture book on Siamese culture, a marble ashtray for Dad, two carved wooden elephants for Mom, bead necklaces for Beulah, finger handcuffs for me, and the grand prize, a gold dagger letter opener for Blaine.

Wooden handle in hand, I was hiding in the coat closet when Blaine arrived home from his summer job as a mason's apprentice, flopped onto the couch, and spread open the Bound Brook Chronicle. Peeking out, I got the bright idea to surprise him by poking the dagger through the newspaper.

"Christ" he screamed as the blade sank into his thigh.

"I didn't mean ..." I whimpered, backing away before taking off out the door with Blaine in hot pursuit. He caught me heading down the driveway and threw me up against the carport wall.

"What were you trying to do?" he hissed, barely restraining his linebacker's wrath.

"I, I, I, I just wanted to surprise you with Beat's present" I blubbered, hot tears streaming down my cheeks.

"You sure did" he laughed as he lowered me down.

Late that night Blaine came into our shared upstairs bedroom and caught me peeking from under the covers.

"D'ya hear that mouse?" he asked letting out a high-pitched fart.

I pinched my eyes closed pretending to be asleep.

"Don't worry about it" he added lying back on his bed, "accidents happen and I'm OK."

A little while later I was jarred awake by a scream. Blaine leapt out of bed and charged down the steps with me right behind. Turning the corner from the top flight we found our father with clenched fists standing over top of Mom who was pinned down on the steps.

"Back off" threatened Blaine crouching slightly on the top step.

"It's none a your bus..." begins Dad, cut off by a flying tackle knocking them both into the living room.

Blaine rolled up and ran out the door. Mom crawled up the stairs sobbing and pushed past me into the bathroom. Dad sat there on the living room floor with head in hands. I just went to bed.

———

The bus slowly pulls out to reveal a couple of guys in military greens standing on the corner waiting for the light to change. Neither one is Blaine. The morning after he took off in the lime-green Cadillac Dad had walked to work at Apgar's to find his dream car parked in the usual spot. When he arrived home in the car that evening we all knew Blaine wouldn't be back.

"Whose troubles?" is all I say to Dad's advice before heading in to watch Rowan and Martin's Laugh-In.

Lesson 17: Lift Your Legs

"The early bird gets the worm" quips Mom offering me the last pancake.

"What about Beulah?" I reply realizing she hasn't been down to eat since the accident two days ago.

———

We had decided to ride our big siblings' bikes because they were both in southeast Asia. Beat was still in Bangkok teaching English and Blaine was somewhere in Vietnam after enlisting in the U.S. Army so he wouldn't have to come home after breaking up Mom and Dad's fight.

I could step up onto Beat's big Schwinn through the girl bar but Beulah had to climb the chain-link fence to hop onto Blaine's English Racer. She was only able to reach one petal at a time and I couldn't reach the seat so we wobbled out onto Hanken Road and turned down Tea Street headed for the park.

Two big black birds hopped down off the Stagecoach as Newsy called out "Where ya goin?"

"Out for a spin on our new bikes" answered Beulah.

"Evergreen Avenue's a good ride off Old Ladies' Hill" he huffed trotting out to the road.

"Why do they call it that?" asked Beulah.

"It was named ... the Evergreens ... by Daniel Talmadge ... who built his mansion ... on the old Codrington foundation."

"No, I meant Old Ladies' Hill."

"Miss Caroline LaMonte ... donated it ... for old people ... after her parents ... died."

"Velly intellesting ... but schtoopit" she quips mimicking Arte Johnson's German soldier from Laugh-In as we rode off.

I stopped at the top of the hill but Beulah circled around unable to get down without a fence.

"What about the dogs?" I asked recalling the two beagles halfway down the hill who chased all passersby.

"Just hold your legs up" she replied turning into the slope.

70

I pushed off behind her and thought I glimpsed one of the little dogs crouching in a yard.

It bolted as Beulah whizzed past with legs held high. The dog let out a yelp as it skidded under the back tire. The big bike flipped up and over as I zipped past. When I finally slowed I looked back up to see my sister lying in the road. Running back, I shook her by the shoulders until she finally woke up.

"Where are we?"

"Old Ladies' Hill."

"My head hurts, let's go home."

———

"Here she is, Miss America" sings Mom two days later, failing to notice Beulah is pale as a ghost with a big knot on her forehead. I pass off the pancake, half a glass of milk, and a small smile of relief.

Lesson 18: Pack It Hard

Sixth grade at LaMonte School is decent until Junior Montana arrives. The Mets are in the Series and Y.A. and Rita Cecchini are in my class. The Monkees are on TV and Mr. Righetti is our first man teacher. He's also the Bound Brook High School football and baseball coach who encourages us to play four way running bases out on the blacktop before school and at recess. I think I'm the fastest trumpet player, math doer, and, most importantly, runner.

"Me run faster den ju muchachos" brags Junior Montana, newly arrived from Puerto Rico.

"Bound Brook's an immigrant town, first Sicilians to work the LaMonte woolen mills, then Poles to factories along the Raritan, now Hispanics" comments Newsy.

"Shut your big Guinea mouth" retorts Mazurk.

"Shit" is all I can muster to Junior's machismo.

He's in the first wave from Central America and he is fast but not around the bases or down the football field. The Spic can talk. The sixth grade girls drift from fortune teller hand games to hear Junior with his curly black hair and dark skin rap. Y.A. coming out with "Cecchini has mucho matteta" is the last straw.

———

A big black bird flaps up from a garbage can as a snowball fight erupts across LaMonte Avenue. We're making our way home from school in an unexpected early December storm.

"Me heat dem for ju, me heat dem for ju" exclaims Junior Montana, exuberant in his first snow.

Seeing his weak lobs plop onto the road I cross the street and start pelting this Junior Montana. He laughs and yells some more until the third hit. Fear flashes across his dark eyes as he ducks behind the can. My chunk of ice arches over a branch and through the wires, clattering the lid before striking him on top of the head. Tears stream down Junior Montana's face as he slumps back toward school. I trudge home oblivious to the joy of that first snow.

———

Junior Montana fades from my life until basketball season. The night before the championship I'm scrambling to finish a book report due the next morning. It had taken a month to summon the courage to ask Mr. Righetti for a recommendation. Hoping for a football or baseball story, I got *The Bronze Bow*. It looked promising at first with its gold Newberry medallion and the possibility of an archery story. By the time I discover it's about two Jewish boys struggling with anger about the Roman occupation it's too late to find another book. Preoccupied with the next day's big game, it takes hours to paraphrase the dust jacket into what I hope will be my own words.

The game is tied as Y.A. leads our fast break offense against Mazurk's tough inside game. With less than a minute to go Mazurk rejects my layup, grabs the loose ball, and takes it up court. We wall him into a corner and he lobs a pass across the lane. Junior Montana takes it in stride and hooks an arching shot that bangs up off the rim and in as time runs out.

Lesson 19: Play Dead

The creaky voice of Melanie singing "I've got a brand new pair of roller skates, you've got a brand new key" floats down the stairway from Diane Albanese's apartment. I'm about to bolt but Jerry Brownell says "rallright Riley Reed" in his best Jetson's voice and heads up for the door.

———

Jerry and I had started hanging out again in eighth grade when my Little League and Pop Warner were done but high school sports had not yet begun. We had already been nailed once that fall. The Army Corps of Engineers was straightening the Middlebrook after tropical storm Doria's flash flood washed out our neighborhood. One night we climbed up into their biggest rig, an earth grader, and found the key in the ignition.

"It's gonna run into the firehouse" I warned, momentarily stopping Jerry from trying to start the thing.

"Nah, it's like my Dad's milk truck" he countered stepping on the clutch and turning the key.

It rumbled to life but stalled before he got it rolling. The second start stuck and the headlights came on showing a black car speeding around the firehouse. He nabbed us as we scrambled down.

———

After our groundings we spend our nights and weekends looking for two things. Jerry expresses one in a song:

> Goddamn Weeds let me set you straight
> your Mama got a cunt like a two-forty-eight
> with hair so long it can mop up floor
> ping pong titties that can bounce off the door.

We find the other on a Sunday when we skip services at the Methodist Church to ride his Kawasaki 75 down an abandoned road in the woods across the brook. Looping trails intersect the half mile blacktop which had been cut off from its counterpart at Calco Park by the building of highway 287, making it a haven for Bound Brook dirt bikers. The best is Bouke Brunk, a 25-year-old Vietnam vet who can ride a wheelie the length of the road or jump its width on his big Ducati.

I'm sitting on a log at the biker's pit pretending to smoke a Marlboro when Jerry zips over.

"Hop on, we got it" he yells over the idling minibike.

He had seen the Ducati lying in the creek at the bottom of a steep hill just past the poop hole. A big black bird flies up off the handlebar as we scramble down and pull out the muddy motorcycle.

"Let's get it outta here before he comes back" urges Jerry.

It takes us an hour to drag the big bike up the hill, another hour to fail at kick starting it, another to fail at push starting. It's getting dark by the time we roll it into the bushes beside Jerry's house. Working on it would have to wait because Diane's mother was going out that night.

———

"Hi guys" greets Diane throwing open the door and hitting a button on the record player. The new 45 from The Who's Tommy album drops down onto the turntable. Her shy and pretty friend Dona Mondrone lights a candle as "See me, feel me..." sweeps the four of us onto the couch.

"Want to hear my new song?" Jerry asks, launching into it before we can answer.

> Ain't your Mama pretty
> she got meatballs in her titty
> she got scrambled egg
> between her leg
> ain't your Mama pretty?

Diane reaches back, hits the lights, slips onto his lap, and plants a wet kiss.
    Dona rolls her eyes and leans away from them and toward me. Our eyes meet with a smile before bumping lips. A giggle out of the way, we hold each other's cheeks and touch puckered lips, then whole lips, then tips of tongues. Mine finds fine hairs at one corner, a groove on top, a slight smile at the other corner, a smooth lower lip. The room fills with sighs, slurps, moans, and jingles and it takes us a moment to decipher that keys

are being fumbled in the door. Then Diane leaps for the light switch, Dona the candle, and Jerry and I the chairs across the room. Mrs. Albanese surveys the scene and says "see you later boys."

————

The sycamore leaves turn tan as Jerry and I either fiddle with the Ducati or meet Diane and Dona down the brook. We make a little fort with a pine needle floor under the bushes beside a back trail. Dona and I are still above the neck but Jerry and Diane are under shirts and heading south fast when winter comes.

On the Saturday before Thanksgiving he calls me on the phone.

"Get over here quick, I figured her out."

I hop on my big black Schwinn with the banana bike handle bars salvaged from the flood and pedal up Tea Street to the American Legion parking lot next to his old tan house. Jerry straddles the motorcycle and reaches down with one hand to spray gas into the ruined carburetor. I push it across the empty blacktop and hop on as he pops the clutch. Our Ducati roars to life, makes three laps around the lot, and is heading for the road when the engine dies, never to fire up again.

Lesson 20: Paint it Black

"Bite this" taunts Harold Johnson stopping in front of my locker on his way to the shower.

Sweat drips from my chin as I look up to find him holding it three feet in front of my face. I drop off the bench into a squat to ram my head into his chest but his sidekick Wayne Henry pushes him away leaving me glaring at a row of red freshmen football lockers.

Harry had been my first African-American friend when we were both legacy players on the Bound Brook Pop Warner little team. His brother Van was carrying the big team to an undefeated season. My brother Blaine was the big team coach. Harry was a fast halfback like his brother but also fumble prone. I was a running quarterback like mine but didn't like tackles.

One Sunday after our little team game Harry had come over to my house for lunch before the big team game.

"Whyn't ya boys get in the house" pled Mom as we took turns returning punts in the yard.

When the pimiento cheese sandwiches and Campbell's tomato soup were ready we wolfed them down and ran back up to LaMonte Field.

"Why'd ya wanna bring that darky here?" asked Mom that night. It was the late sixties and race riots in nearby Newark were still a fresh fear for the all white town. A handful of black families lived across the river in South Bound Brook and most people liked it that way. The twin boroughs had separate schools until high school but Harry and I remained football friends until he was ineligible in 8th grade.

———

The locker room encounter happens after our last practice before the first freshmen football game. Coach Dan Gramicelli had Harry pegged as starting halfback like his brother who's now the star on a varsity team which had gone 8-0-1 the previous season. I'm relegated to kick returner and defensive cornerback.

Neither Harry nor I liked the one-on-one tackling drills in which a runner tries to get by a defender between two blocking dummies. He avoided being hit by lulling defenders into not trying with a jog and a dance, then racing by. I did it by a flat out sprint past the slow tacklers or by steam-rolling into the faster ones before they could run into me. That day in practice a big black bird circled overhead as I faced up against Harry. He started his jogging dance and I charged through it, hitting him hard with my helmet and knocking the ball loose. This spearing is illegal

82

but Danny Gram had taught us to avoid the penalty by hitting face first instead of with the top of the helmet. A single tear slipped from Harry's eye as he fell back holding his belly. Then he sat up laughing and dropped to the back of the line.

———

After his buddy diffuses Harry's locker room taunt I quickly dress without showering and walk home looking over my shoulder. My trembling finally stops when I drink a cool dipperful from the well at Patullo's greenhouse.

The next afternoon my feet freeze as the opening kickoff descends but a glimpse of tacklers charging down the field thaws my legs for a return to midfield.

"Way to go Weeds, that's a thirty yarder" calls Newsy keeping statistics on the sideline.

"You're done" says Harry jabbing a finger at me as he joins the offense and I leave the field.

Two plays later he takes off around left end, cuts back across the field, and scampers in for a beautiful fifty yard touchdown run.

On the kickoff we nail the Bernardsville runner deep in their territory. Then they start moving the ball down the field on power sweeps in which a pulling guard and fullback lead the halfback around one end of the row of linemen. It's first down and ten yards to go for a first down at midfield when I read a sweep developing around right end. I scoot past their big pulling guard and pop up into their halfback. Grabbing his jersey for dear life, we're both driven back by a swarm of tacklers. Our safety rams the pile helmet first cracking me on the point of the left elbow.

An electric shock shoots through me as I stumble in circles and fall to the packed dirt. Memory fades until I come-to kicking and screaming because they're strapping my right arm down for surgery. The nurses wrestle me back to bed, reassuring that the right arm is for an IV but only the fractured left elbow will be operated on.

Both freshmen and varsity teams go on to undefeated seasons behind the running of the Johnson brothers. I'm secretly relieved to be watching from the sideline but Blaine assures me I'll play next year. Those metal pins sticking out of my medial epicondyle whisper a comforting no.

Lesson 21: Ride the Snake

"Come out and you'll be quarterback" proposes Heinze DiGiampaolo catching me outside sophomore chemistry class. He's the team captain and all-conference linebacker for the Bound Brook Crusaders.

———

After the pins were removed from my fractured freshmen ulna I had determined to become a runner. Donning Blaine's old track shorts, I had taken off down Tea Street for a training loop around Calco Park. Chest pain before reaching the softball field shattered my assumption that cross country runners were just not tough enough to play football.

I should have known better because I could never catch Dicky Dick in laps before and after Pop Warner practice. He was to become a freshman cross country phenom and all-state sophomore for BBHS. The summer before our junior year he was wooed away to a Catholic track school while I was running sprints, lifting weights, and throwing passes for a return to Bound Brook football.

———

One of the reasons I agree to go back out is that the quarterback is kept out of tackling during practices. But the night before the first game I'm terrified as a 5'9" 150 pound fifteen-year-old about to face hirsute seventeen and eighteen-year-old guys. After dinner I head down the park and the jocks are milling around the basketball courts, the freaks in the playground in a haze of cigarette smoke.   I head for the courts where the pretty little sister of one of the seniors is laughing as my teammates tease her.

"Hey Monty, what's jailbait doing down the park" quips Heinze.

"None of your bee's wax" she shoots back.

"C'mon, we're goin up to the Statues" yells Mazurk from over among the freaks.

"Let's go Weeds" offers Heinze as a group piles into his pink Chevy Vega.

I hop into the backseat and that freshman girl tumbles in next to me. As we climb Mountain Avenue and catch a view of the lights down in the Raritan valley she starts to cower. Then she hits the floor as we turn onto Hillcrest Drive.

86

"I hate the mountains" she whines.

"It's all right" I whisper hoping the guys don't see as I touch her shoulder.

The encased sculptures appear in the headlights as we approach what looks like a flaming haunted house.

"This is the studio and kiln of the famous art deco artist Waylande Gregory" calls Newsy leaning out the window of the freak car.

"Let's see one" decides Heinze as the seniors jump out and start hacking at the burlap and plastic wrapped around the nearest statue.

"Why do they call you Monty?" I ask as she hangs onto my knee.

"My dumb mother named me after Dad's Mom."

"Your grandmother's named Monty?"

"No silly, Caroline LaMonte and I hate Neil Diamond."

Just then a head of wild white hair appears in a window of the low stucco house. By the time the old lady throws open the door we're peeling away. The headlights flash across the partially uncovered sculpture of a mermaid going down on a snake-entwined man.

Later that night after snapping off a toothbrush in my mouth and then tossing and turning for hours, I finally fall asleep remembering Monty's smile as we came down off First Watchung.

———

In the locker room before the game I'm hoping no one can see my trembling. Pulling up the red undershorts which had helped me to a starting position in sophomore baseball calms me a little. Slipping on a new left elbow pad stops the shaking. Strapping on my brother Blaine's old high top spikes makes me feel ready to run.

"Let me see your cleats" commands the referee walking up during warm-ups.

He declares the three-quarter inch spikes illegal so I have to borrow Tommy Greenwood's old red and white Riddell soccer shoes.

My legs feel weightless without the heavy black boots as I crouch behind the center for the opening snap. A couple of up the middle runs out of the way, Coach Righetti sends in a quarterback keeper on third down and six. I take the snap and fake a pitchout to the left before turning back around right end. Sprinting past the crashing defensive end I find myself floating down an open field. The cornerback walls me into the sideline so I leap, clipping his shoulder with a foot and tumbling forward a couple of yards. A cheer erupts from the stands as I jog back to the huddle.

"Never leave your feet" shouts the coach.

"Way to go Wiley Reed" is the last thing I hear before joining the huddle, picking out Monty's clear voice over the din.

Three plays later I scoot in for the first score.

On our next series we set them up with fullback runs and halfback pitchouts for small gains. Then Mr. Righetti calls for a flag pattern pass off of a fake quarterback keeper. I clear the defensive end to see our speedy flanker streaking toward the corner of the endzone and no defender within ten yards. My rushed pass falls short by those same ten yards.

Then the rain settles in. Two hours later the mudbowl ends in a 6-6 tie for both points and fumbles. I'm mortified that three of the lost balls were mine.

"As a quarterback you make a pretty good runner" quips Coach Righetti.

Lesson 22: Drive South

"Can I take the Impala by myself around the block to pick up Tommy Greenwood?" I ask on the night of my seventeenth birthday.

"Sure, just be back by midnight" my father replies tossing me the keys.

———

The car had been Beulah's until she went away to Montclair State College that fall. I'd been riding around in Tommy's Comet since he had gotten his license over the summer. We mostly cruised on a loop between the park, McDonalds in Middlesex, and Burger King in Manville with the cassette player blaring Blue Oyster Cult and an occasional six-pack of Schlitz. The driving age in New Jersey was seventeen and a half but you could get a learner's permit on your birthday.

————

I back out of the carport, turn down Hanken Road, and drive right past Tommy's house in the circle and out the other end of the loop.

"You got it" beams Monty sashaying down from their big house in Piedmont Farms.

She pops onto the bench seat and scoots over close as I drive away with my right arm over her shoulder.

"How about up in the mountains?" I ask as she wraps herself around my chest.

"Pull over where it's dark" she urges as we approach the unlit north end of Church Street.

We flop into the backseat in a tangle of pants and shirts. The windows steam up as we pull over a blanket, tear open a Trojan, and settle in for our first long slow ride.

————

"Pediddle" she laughs, turning my head for a kiss as a VW beetle with a single headlight passes.

I gladly oblige while cruising slowly down Maple Avenue.

90

"What'll you do after school?" she asks.

"Newsy and I are checking out this small college down in Virginia."

"What happens then?"

"They have a good history program for him and pre-med for me."

"No, where does your going away leave me?"

"A six-hour drive away" satisfies her for now.

I'm turning left onto Vosseller when a car coming the other way pulls into the intersection. Monty screams as we screech to a halt missing a collision by inches.

"What the hell?" screams the guy hopping out of his car.

I shrug and drive away as he flips us the bird.

———

"How was your night drivin?" asks my father from his bed as I float in right on time.

"No sweat" I lie dropping the keys on the dresser and bounding up the stairs.

He never asks about the small burgundy stain forever on the middle of the backseat of the sky blue Impala.

Lesson 23: Keep Your Feet

"Run like they're chuckin spears" yells Coach Righetti as I take the field as a senior halfback with the Bound Brook High School offense. It must show that I'm clueless because Newsy who's keeping statistics on the sideline whispers "Yo Weeds, just get away from those black dudes."

———

It's the last game of the season against our traditional rival the Somerville Pioneers in their black and orange uniforms. The predominantly African-American team is the current Somerset County champion and heavily favored to win the Thanksgiving morning game. The Bound Brook Crusaders are an all white team but only because we had lost Harold Johnson and Wayne Henry during freshmen year when one of the black tennis players was suspended from school for refusing to cut his afro before the first match. The next morning most of the black students, Harry among them, boycotted school by standing out on the front lawn as classes started. His big brother Van arrived with the suspended tennis player and they convinced everyone to go back into school. Harry burst into study hall and strode down the aisle with eyes darting back and forth. We all watched as he hopped over a row of seats to stand over a guy we all knew was dealing pot in the boys' room between classes. As the guy stood up Harry clocked him in the mouth with a quick right jab. In what seemed like slow motion the guy fell back over the seat with blood dribbling from his lip. Harry turned to leave and bumped into the pretty and popular German teacher attending study hall that morning.

"Harold, what's going on?" she asked with a bewildered look.

He responded with a big grin and a quick two-handed squeeze before Wayne hustled him out of the auditorium. That was the last we saw of both Harry and Wayne.

———

Three years later the Thanksgiving game starts ominously for Bound Brook as Harry's cousin Lester Jones returns the opening kickoff in snow flurries all the way for a Somerville touchdown. Then the defenses take over, shutting down running plays on the icy field. On one of ours I try stiff-arming their linebacker to break around end into the open field. It's hard to read his dark face as he leans toward me at full tilt so I ram a straightened left arm into his facemask to push off. He reaches through and wraps up my legs, giving my foot a sharp twist before rolling away.

Late in the second quarter the sun emerges and the Pioneers start moving the ball downfield on short passes. It feels like they're ready to steamroll us until Mazurk breaks through from defensive end and tips the ball as its being thrown. Heinze picks it off and I take the field with our offense to the coach's spear chucker admonition and Newsy's translation.

———

Our first play is a power sweep to the right. I field the pitch from our quarterback and take off behind the pulling guard Tommy Greenwood who cuts down their defensive end. Turning the corner I see the field open up all the way to the endzone and burst forward as Lester Jones sprints across the field to try to catch me.

"He's at the fifty yard line, the forty, the thirty, twenty..." calls Newsy from the sideline.

My brother Blaine, just back from Vietnam, is running down the track alongside the field on the Bound Brook side. Harry Johnson is standing near the goal line on the Somerville side with hands jammed into his overcoat pockets and a smile in his eyes. My sister Beulah is standing on tiptoes on the rail along the top of the bleachers. Monty is jumping up and down with the BBHS cheerleaders. A big black bird caws from up on the goalpost as Lester closes in. He dives at the five yard line and grabs my left foot. My spike rips off into his hands as we tumble forward and land in a twisting heap.

Lesson 24: Break the Ice

"The short-stemmed glass is for cognac, the long one for champagne" instructs Monty as she drags me up the flagstone walkway.

"OK but we leave right after dinner, right?" I beg.

———

I had resisted going to her house all Fall but caved in to her request from under the mistletoe at the Chimney Rock Inn. Her family's ten acre property was imposing with a wrought-iron fence topped with spikes and a latched gate. The big house was barely visible from the road, tucked behind a grove of rhododendron and pines. The front columns, wooden shakes painted bright white, kelly green shutters, and matching servant house clearly marked it as out of bounds for the rest of us. A strange American flag with three stripes and eleven stars circling a central one is flapping in the cold breeze from a low pole in the middle of the front yard.

———

"Welcome to Piedmont Farm" greets a tuxedo-clad old man as we step into a marble-floored foyer. "May I take your coat?"

I'm sweating as I hand over my varsity double B jacket and Monty ushers me into the dining room.

"Caroline deah, who's come to suppah?" smiles an elegant elderly woman reaching for my hand.

"Grandma Caroline, this is Wiley Reed" Monty answers. "He's the captain of the Bound Brook football team."

"Mah oh mah, we haven't had a genuwine hero in the Kern household since the Wah of Northen Agression" the old lady drawls. "What does yah fatha do?"

"Isn't it time for the aperitif?" Monty asks sparing me a lie.

The meal proceeds with smoked oysters, a whole pineapple-glazed ham carved at the table, biscuits with red eye gravy, succotash, corn pudding, and rounds of sweet tea for the house.

"Heyah's to old Virginia" toasts Grandmother LaMonte draining her champagne and holding out the glass for more.

"Here, here" I join in disliking the bubbles but enjoying the buzz.

"Wiley deah, did Caroline tell ya'll about Wheatland?"

"Newsy knew" I marvel holding up my empty glass.

"Newport News was wheyah the Kerns first arrived but Wheatland was the family plantation in Romney" she continues. "They knew right off that Fahtha was a Yankee when he pronounced the u in Staunton Normal School. That's wheah he taught mah mutha Rebecca Kern, bless her teenaged heart."

"No shit?" I let slip.

"Grandfatha Kern built our western estate for the so-called newlaweds" she laughs with a wink.

"I might be going to college in Virginia" I offer hoping she didn't spot my reddening cheeks and quick glance at Monty.

"Keep an eye out for our lost Wheatland, won't ya deah?"

"Yes ma'am" I oblige.

"Grandma, we've got to get going to Zab's New Year's party" interjects Monty to my relief.

———

A blast of arctic air greets our departure from the LaMonte mansion.

"Can we go skating on New Year's day?" Monty asks.

"Yeah but I can't wait to tell Newsy."

"He can come too" she suggests.

The next morning Newsy plops into the blue Impala next to Monty who's snuggled up close to me. We cross the Queen's Bridge over the Raritan and drive through South Bound Brook headed to Colonial Park.

"Hey Newsy, did you know George LaMonte was a high school teacher who married his rich student?" I gloat to Monty's giggle as we pull into the lot next to a frozen lake.

"Yeah but the Fleishman distillery and estate was here" he answers. "The family donated their house and land for the park when they took their operations to Kentucky to be closer to the corn."

The new ice reflects a brilliant blue of the winter sky as Newsy wraps up in a blanket and sits beside us with a smile. Monty and I don our skates, hers new white figure skates with pom-poms hanging from the back, mine Blaine's old brown hockey skates two sizes too big. Hand-in-hand we step onto the ice and glide in one smooth stroke all the way across the glassy lake, laughing all the way.

Lesson 25: Hit the Hole

"Just aim for that dark spot beside the rock" coaxes Mazurk from below, still dripping from his plunge into the Middlebrook. Newsy and I glance at each other and step to the edge of Buttermilk Falls.

———

We had climbed Chimney Rock on the last day of summer before Newsy and I went away to college. Sweat trickled into our eyes as we looked out across the gorge to the plains of the Raritan river valley.

"General Washington stood here and saw Cornwallis march down the Old York Road to Princeton" commented Newsy.

"I can piss all the way to Princeton" laughed Mazurk from up on the whitewashed rock.

"Princeton would be cool" continued Newsy "but Randolph-Macon has colloquy."

"College, schmollege" groaned Mazurk, "let's go swimming."

"Blaine said we can bypass the no-trespassing signs and barbed wire down this trail" I chipped in heading north down the rocky slope.

Halfway down the roar of the falls emerged over the background buzz of seventeen year cicadas.

———

"These falls are the spillway for the old Bound Brook Water Company reservoir" mumbles Newsy as we look down into the green water.

"Yeah, didn't the flashboards wash out to cause the flood?" I ask.

"That was Elizabethtown's new reservoir on the north fork and it was tropical storm Doria that made the Middlebrook and Raritan overflow."

"What was Elizabethtown doing in Bound Brook?"

"They bought up all the small town systems between Jersey City and the Raritan watershed when the Passaic River became too polluted."

"Stealing our water for the New York sprawl?"

102

"Yeppur, they even built two big reservoirs on the Raritan headwaters. Spruce Run was an excavation of a little tributary but all they had to do for Round Valley was pump in the river."

"Velly intellesting" I laugh.

"The state geologists said the circular valley was an eroded volcano but an old picture before the water looked more like an impact crater."

"Quit stalling you goddamn pussies" curses Mazurk from down below.

Three big black birds caw noisily from an overhanging hemlock as Newsy eyes the twenty foot drop, spots the darkness of the deep hole, and leaps, breaking the surface with a huge splash.

"Your turn Weeds" he gasps popping up from the hole.

My knees are trembling as I stare down into the blackness between the rocks.

"Weeds, Weeds, he's our man" cheer Newsy and Mazurk from the rocks below in imitation of BBHS cheerleaders, "if he can't do it, nobody can."

I take a big breath, gaze downstream, and leap.

The cool air whooshes past as I see the Middlebrook tumbling beside the old tank trails, below the eroding breastworks, around a lost Lenape mound, and spilling into the brown Raritan forever flowing, flowing back to the sea.

Lesson 26: Go Home

"What's up Newsy?"

"Yo Mazurk, just back from Randy-Mac for the summer."

"What can I do ya for?"

"Just a Schlitz for old time's sake. When did you start tending at the Rock?"

"I was hangin out here last winter and they needed help. Did ya see him that day?"

"I saw him staring off on the way down."

"Yeah, watchin those goddamn crows instead of the hole."

"Only one was a crow. The others were a southern coastal fish crow and a northern mountain raven. These Watchungs may be the only place where the three ranges overlap."

"Bad news for the crow and Weeds."

"Yeah, but bad news is good for Enzo Januzzi. I'm studying corvid behavior in the Blue Ridge for my colloquy next year."

"No shit, Sherlock? That wiley sombitch scored three that day."

"That he did but it was your tip that turned the tide in the Somerville game."

"Did they ever find him?"

"Nah, our old friend Weeds must still be out there swimming with the green eels."

Newsy's Notes

Binder A, Geis G, Bruce DD. *Juvenile Delinquency: Historical, Cultural and Legal Perspective, 3rd Ed.* Anderson Publishing, Cincinnati, OH 2001.

Bobrick B. *Angel in the Whirlwind: The Triumph of the American Revolution.* Penquin Books, New York 1997.

Carlisle R. *Water Ways.* Elizabethtown Water Company, Elizabeth, NJ 1982.

Carson R, Lear L. *Chesapeake eels seek the Sargasso Sea* in *Lost Woods: The Discovered Writing of Rachel Carson.* Beacon Press, Boston 1999.

Davis TE. *First Houses of Bound Brook.* Washington Campground Association, Bound Brook, NJ 1981.

Echelbarger GL. *We Are In For It: The First Battle of Kernstown.* White Mane Publishing, Shippensburg, PA 1997.

Haynes W. *Dyes Made in America 1915-1940.* Calco Chemical Division, American Cyanamid Company, Bound Brook, NJ.

Heinrich B. *Ravens in Winter.* Summit Books, New York 1989.

Prince CE. *Middlebrook: The American Eagle's Nest.* Somerset County Historical Society, Bridgewater, NJ 1958.

Savage C. *Crows.* Greystone Books, Vancouver 2005.

Schweid R. *Consider the Eel.* University of North Carolina Press, Chapel Hill 2002.

Stratford DA, McKay M. *Images of America: Bound Brook.* Arcadia Publishing, Charleston, SC 2000.

The WPA Guide to 1930s New Jersey. Rutgers University Press 1986.

Weslager CA. *The Delaware Indians: A History.* Rutgers University Press 1972.

Acknowledgements

This book was developed with the support and interest of my siblings Jim, Karen, Alan, Bob, Kathy and Karla Beatty. Many thanks are extended to my friends in our hometown of Bound Brook, New Jersey who made growing up there the lesson of a lifetime. I wish to thank the staff at the Bound Brook Memorial Library who helped to ferret out obscure facts about the town's history. Lastly, I'd like to offer my undying thanks to my chief editor and head cheerleader Mary Essig-Beatty for enduring the many early renditions of the stories in Delinquency Lessons.

About the Author

David Essig-Beatty is a teacher and osteopathic physician in the Allegheny Mountains of southeastern West Virginia. His previous books include *Manipulation at Home: Exercises Based on Osteopathic Structural Examination* (WVSOM 2003), *A Pocket Manual of OMT: Osteopathic Manipulative Treatment for Physicians* (co-author, Lippincott Williams & Wilkins 2006), and *Manipulation in Motion* (co-author, WVSOM DVD 2008). *Delinquency Lessons* is his first work of fiction.

www.ingramcontent.com/pod-product-compliance
Lightning Source LLC
Chambersburg PA
CBHW030637130626

46552CB00002B/889